LIFE
WENT
ON
ANYWAY

Life Went On Anyway

Stories

Oleg Sentsov

Translated from the Russian by Uilleam Blacker

Deep Vellum Publishing

Dallas, Texas

Deep Vellum
3000 Commerce St., Dallas, Texas 75226
deepvellum.org · @deepvellum

Deep Vellum is a 501c3 nonprofit literary arts organization
founded in 2013 with the mission to bring
the world into conversation through literature.

First edition, 2019

ISBNs: 978-1-941920-87-9 (paperback) | 978-1-941920-88-6 (ebook)

LIBRARY OF CONGRESS CONTROL NUMBER: 2019947672

The translation of this book was carried out within the PEN Ukraine
Translation Fund Grants program in cooperation with the International
Renaissance Foundation.

Cover Design by Anna Zylicz | annazylicz.com
Interior Layout and Typesetting by Kirby Gann

Text set in Bembo, a typeface modeled on typefaces cut by Francesco Griffo
for Aldo Manuzio's printing of *De Aetna* in 1495 in Venice

Printed in the United States of America on acid-free paper.

CONTENTS

Translator's Introduction

Oleg Sentsov was catapulted into the news headlines in 2014 for all the wrong reasons. He was working on a new film. It had a bigger budget than any of his previous projects and could have represented his step up from promising new-comer to established figure on the European cinematic stage. He was an unusual and uncategorizable figure in Ukrainian culture: a filmmaker, writer and dramatist, not restricted to any one genre, nor, as a Russian-speaking, ethnically Russian, Ukrainian patriot from Crimea, easily labelled. But his star was on the rise. His film, literary, and theater projects were getting more and more ambitious. Then in his late 30s, it seemed that Sentsov's time was just beginning.

But it wasn't any of this that made him really famous. In 2013 and early 2014, Ukrainians took to the streets in huge numbers, determined to wrest their country free from its corrupt elites and set it on a course towards Europe, stability, and dignity, in what became known as the Euromaidan protests (the name comes from *Maidan nezalezhnosti*, Independence Square, the central square in Kyiv that was the epicenter of the movement). The Kremlin, which liked to keep as close a hold as possible over those same elites, and over Ukraine as a whole, was enraged and alarmed at the obstinacy of its neighbour, whose people refused to be cowed, neither by the manipulations of political technologists and propaganda, nor by brute force. Russia hit Ukraine at its weakest points: in Crimea and the eastern region of Donbas, where the protests had the least momentum.

The annexation of Crimea was carried out with speed, before Ukraine had time to realize what was happening. Soldiers in unmarked uniforms occupied the peninsula, overran its parliament and forced through legislation for a referendum at gunpoint. The official result showed a remarkable 97 percent in favour of joining Russia, on an 83 percent turnout—remarkable for a previously politically apathetic region that had voted (albeit narrowly) in favour of Ukrainian independence only twenty-three years previously.

What happened in eastern Ukraine was even worse. The Kremlin created dubious "separatist" movements in the Donetsk and Luhansk regions, pieced together from imported Russian secret service agents and local pro-Russian activists and criminal elements. Russian troops, disguised as rebels and volunteers, soon followed, accompanied by formidable military hardware. A region that had never had a political separatist movement to speak of suddenly had not only a movement, but a powerful army that was capable of fending off the Ukrainian Armed Forces. In the following years, thousands of Ukrainians, military and civilians, as well as Russian troops, would die in a protracted conflict.

The Euromaidan movement was far from shunned in Crimea or the east, however. The big cities in eastern Ukraine had their own "*maidans*." Oleg Sentsov was one of many Crimeans who threw themselves into the protests. He dropped work on his movie and returned to the peninsula to help organize protests and to bring food and supplies to Ukrainian sailors trapped in their Crimean bases. He got noticed, and not only by his fellow activists. From the earliest days of the occupation, fear and intimidation have been key tools for the "new authorities." Always keen to make examples of local activists in order to tame dissent, the FSB (the Russian secret services, formerly the KGB) arrested Sentsov in May 2014 and took him to Russia, where, despite never having applied for or been granted Russian citizenship, he was tried as a Russian citizen.

The FSB came up with the following story: Sentsov was a member of a nationalist terrorist organisation, and he and his co-conspirators had been planning a series of attacks on various targets in Crimea; they had set fire to the doorway of the headquarters of Putin's United Russia party in Simferopol, and they had planned to blow up a Lenin monument. The charges of terrorism carried potential sentences of twenty years. Sentsov was repeatedly interrogated and, he says, tortured in order to make him confess: according to his testimony, he was beaten, suffocated, and threatened with rape and death. He didn't confess.

The trial was a farce. The FSB initially found no evidence at his home, but on a second visit "uncovered" explosives they somehow hadn't noticed before. As proof of Sentsov's extremist views, they presented a copy of a film called *Everyday Fascism* that they had found among his DVDs. The film (often translated into English as *Triumph Over Violence*), by the Soviet director Mikhail Romm, is one of the most famous anti-fascist films ever made. But the point was never to make a convincing case against Sentsov. It was to orchestrate a classic show trial, designed to show dissenters that the normal rule of law no longer applied, and that if they wanted to get you, they would, crime or no crime, evidence or no evidence.

Sentsov's performance—and the word is a good one in this context—in the courtroom was a powerful demonstration of dignity in the face of tyranny. He steadfastly refused to play along: he denied all charges, refused to show fear, and treated the whole spectacle with bemused contempt. He undermined the neo-colonial violence of the whole situation by telling the court, in reference to the denial of his Ukrainian citizenship, "I am not a serf: I cannot be transferred with the land." His final speech after being sentenced to twenty years was a work of art in itself. Refusing to dignify the absurdities of his own trial with a response, he chose to speak about Russia. He cited the famous line from Mikhail Bulgakov's *Master and Margarita* that "the greatest sin on earth is cowardice," and criticized the Russian elites who were complicit in or silent about state-sponsored abuses for the sake of their careers and wealth. He recognized that there were many Russians who knew that things were wrong and wished them the courage to overcome their fear and stand up against oppression, just as Ukrainians had done in the months prior.

Sentsov's appeals went largely unheard in Russia, but they were heard at home and around the world. He became a symbol of the Russian state's cynical disregard for human dignity and basic human rights. In 2018 he spent an awe-inspiring 145 days on hunger strike, protesting not for his own release, but for the release of every one of the seventy-odd Ukrainian political prisoners, many from Crimea, who were then held in Russian jails (the number at the time of writing is close to one hundred). He refused to ask for clemency, and when his mother did so on his behalf, he urged her not to. Remarkably, Sentsov continued to write while in prison. He had occasional visitors, though the Russian state often made this difficult. It was possible to communicate with him via email: you sent a message in Russian via the prison system website, paid a small fee, and within a couple of weeks a reply came, a scanned copy of a hastily handwritten note. The messages were censored, so you couldn't say anything political, but you could discuss professional matters—publications, translations, this book. He was courteous, sometimes funny, even cheerful, in his replies, and business-like when it cames to his work.

In early September 2019, just when this book was about to go to press, Oleg Sentsov was unexpectedly released as part of a prisoner exchange between Ukraine and Russia. Thirty-five Ukrainian political prisoners arrived on a flight from Moscow and emerged into the Kyiv sunlight to cheers from waiting families and journalists. Sentsov looked well, though he had gone a little grey since his trial five years earlier. He said little on the tarmac to the massed journalists, but he did say a few words. Just as he had done when he went on hunger strike, his priority was not to speak about himself, but about the dozens of Ukrainian political prisoners who remain in Russia: "Even after the last of them is released," he said, "our struggle will still not be over."

•

The stories in this volume were published in Kyiv, in Russian, in 2015, when Sentsov was already in prison. This book was his second, after the novel *Kupite knigu, ona smeshnaia* (*Buy the Book, It's Funny*, 2014). It turns out that one of the texts, "Autobiography," wasn't really meant to be included, as it was actually written as part of an application for a directing course. But now that it's out, Oleg is happy for you to read it. The stories are funny, at once warm and bleak; they betray simultaneously unashamed emotion and bone-dry irony. They are painfully and hilariously revealing about life in the twilight years of the Soviet Union and the difficult post-Soviet years: a life that was hard, one that should never be sentimentalized, but which nevertheless had its own moments of beauty if you knew where to look—and Oleg knows where to look.

On the one hand, these stories throw up all kinds of challenges for the translator—the everyday realia of life in Soviet Crimea, for example, are not easily transferable into English, and Sentsov's tone, which slides from street-wise informality into moments of poetry, always keeps you on your toes. Yet Sentsov also writes with an easy, flowing familiarity that, once you have tuned in to it, seems to simply carry you along, and the stories sometimes felt like they were translating themselves.

I hope the readers of these stories will think about Oleg Sentsov the political prisoner, as well as all the other Ukrainian political prisoners, many of them from Crimea, who remain in Russian jails. I hope they will tell their friends about them and the injustice that they have suffered in Russia. But I hope they will also appreciate Oleg Sentsov the artist, and that these translations can help them see the world through his eyes.

Life Went On Anyway

Autobiography (in Literary Form)

I was born on Monday the 13th. I guess that's why I've had such a fun life.

My childhood was like any childhood, a happy time. I grew up in a village, in a semi-educated family: my mother was a nursery school teacher, my father a driver. We didn't have much money, but I have only good memories.

I did well in school, was top of the class. I read a lot. Did my homework, but wasn't a swot, I got by with a good memory and a thirst for knowledge. I was an outsider in my class. Skinny. I got beat up.

When I was twelve I got a really bad cold. It led to complications with my legs, I developed polyarthritis and they were paralyzed. After half a year of treatment, I started walking again.

In my final years in high school I would argue with my

teachers, sometimes on the topic we were discussing, sometimes just out of insolence—I can't stand people who think they're smarter than everyone else but really aren't. I began to fit in better at school with the cool kids, started to hang out with the troublemakers, and life started to take on new dimensions. I got into sports, although the doctors warned against it. Medicine gave up on me, and I gave up on it. I got stronger and tougher.

After school I moved to the city of S. to study at university, a prestigious institution, and applied for a state-funded place. They didn't want to accept my documents:

"Where are you from, son?"

"From the village of S."

"Did you finish school with a gold medal?"

"No."

"Silver?"

"No."

"So what do want from us?"

"To study!"

So I studied independently. Scraped by with the bare minimum grades. The happiest day of my life. But half a year later I got disillusioned: the students pretended to study, and the teachers pretended to teach. I gave up on attending classes. Did just enough to pass everything. I had a good time. I hung out with rockers and musicians. It was fun. I had no money, but it was fun. Things will never be like that again.

I finished my studies. I didn't try to find a job in my specialization (marketing). Nine-to-five wasn't for me. I'd have murdered all my coworkers by the end of the working day.

When I was twenty, my father died (I was only able to start talking about it ten years later). My carefree days were over. I had been doing odd jobs here and there since I was about thirteen, but now I really had to start earning. I worked at the market. I sold Herbalife products for a year, ripped people off. I started my own business with a friend. I borrowed a lot of money and got in too deep, my friend disappeared. But I survived. That was 1996.

I worked as an administrator in computer clubs, and then as a manager. I got into gaming. I played online video games professionally for four years. I took part in competitions, became the champion of Ukraine. I traveled a bit. I created my own gaming team, my own website, gathered like-minded people around me, and now I'm the leader of the Crimean gaming movement.

The last year and a half I've been busy setting up the biggest internet center in Simferopol. I did it. Business is good.

When I was twenty, I wanted a lot of money. I didn't have any, and I just couldn't earn any. By the time I turned thirty my worldview had changed completely, and money was no longer so important in my system of values, but I had it . . . I guess that's how things should be. I don't know.

A bit about my personal life: for more than ten years I've been living with the same woman. I'm married to her. I have two little kids with her. I love them all.

•

I never dreamed of becoming a filmmaker. But I've loved movies since I was a kid. Good movies. The older I got, the more I educated myself about films, and the more refined my cinematic tastes became. The more I matured, the circle of people I could talk to about films narrowed. Today, there are only two or three of them left.

•

I've always read books. A lot of books. At school I wrote essays. Always got top marks for them. After I got into gaming, I started writing articles about it, my thoughts just built up inside me, I couldn't hold them back. And as my beloved Mikhal Mikhalych Zhvanetsky used to say, "Writing is like pissing, you should do it only when you can no longer hold it in." I no longer had the will to hold it in; all I had was the will to write. At first, it all came out wrong somehow, though it was fun. After writing about ten articles, I had refined my technique and found my own style. I wrote a couple of stories or essays—I don't really know what to call them myself. Now I'm writing a book.

I want to make films. My thoughts are building up again, and paper just isn't as expressive as celluloid. I'm trying to get into a directing course. It seems like this is a pretty good one. If I don't get in, then I'll go ahead anyway, on my own, without any preparation— it won't be the first time.

I don't like Boris Grebenshchikov much, but he once said something interesting in answer to a question about his musical education: "Thirty years of listening to music and twenty years of playing it." I've been watching movies for thirty years—time to move forward.

Dog

When I was a child, I wanted to have a dog. A German shepherd. Definitely a German shepherd. I saw them a lot in movies, and there were a couple in our village. I wanted my own. To take it for walks, to train it. To walk along the street and have everyone look at me. I wanted it to obey me, I wanted us to love each other.

I had already had a dog once before. It was more of a family dog, not really mine. It had an entirely unheroic name—Tuzik. He was a black mongrel, medium-sized, who one day just wandered into our yard. Tuz (as I called him, to make him seem a bit more serious, mostly in my own eyes) had clearly had a rough time—you could tell he'd been beaten and abused plenty. His first week with us he spent inside his kennel and didn't come out even to eat. He was so happy that nobody was hurting him, and he easily preferred peace and quiet to eating.

But later Tuzik got used to us, we all grew to love him. I was about nine or ten years old then. I took him for walks in the forest, in the fields. I walked him on a rope. At home he was chained up, but at night we let him go, and he ran around the garden or even in the street and didn't bother anybody. Tuz was really smart, obedient, and good-natured. But his past life had left a mark on him. They say that people's life experience can be read in their faces. It's true. But a dog's life can be read in its eyes. That black mongrel's eyes were sad for good.

A few years passed, and one ordinary morning my mum woke me up, sat on the edge of my bed, and told me that Tuzik had been killed. They were going around shooting stray dogs, and they had shot him, early in the morning, in the street right by the gates to our house. My mum suggested I should cry a bit, it would make me feel better, but I couldn't. I couldn't believe it. No, I knew that he'd been shot, but I neither believed nor understood it.

That's how it always is. A certain period of time always has to pass between the moment when you're told that a loved one has died and the moment when you understand it and feel the loss. It's happened to me a few times. When I turned twenty and a man came and told me that my father had died, the first sensation I had, which filled up my entire mind, was "it's not possible." And even an hour later, when I saw him lying there as though he were asleep, I didn't feel the loss. And when they carried him out of the house in his coffin the next day, somewhere I felt a sharp pain, but there was no all-consuming grief. The next time I felt the dull pain was when a man at the cemetery, after telling the family to say goodbye to the deceased, gave the instruction to close the coffin, and they began to hammer, with dull, very dull blows, on the lid, in which they'd already stuck the nails in preparation. In the deep grave lay an empty bottle, forgotten by the gravediggers after they'd drunk its contents.

It felt like everything was happening in a cotton-wool dream. Like it's not happening to you. The wake at the workers' canteen, the vodka that doesn't make you drunk, and all those people, random or sympathetic observers, various relatives.

And then, late in the evening, when everything had calmed down, when only close family were left in the house, when the cleaning up had been finished and we were getting ready for bed after the hard day, in a quiet place on the veranda, in the darkness, beyond the edge of the circle of light drawn by the street lamp in the yard, I sat down on a small, portable bench. I was very tired and sat in silence, staring into the darkness. And then I understood that I was sitting in the very place where my father used to like to sit. I was sitting on his favorite bench, the one he'd made himself. And then I distinctly and clearly understood that he was gone. I felt it physically—here's his place, here's his bench, but he's not here, and he's never coming back. It was frightening to feel this emptiness, this blackness. And I started to cry, quietly, slowly, not making a sound. My eight-year-old nephew was standing nearby and noticed that I was crying. He tried to comfort me, like kids do—he started stroking my head. Not making a sound. And I sat on the bench, with my head bowed, silently crying, and he stood next to me and silently stroked my head.

After Tuzik died, almost a year passed. I persuaded my parents to get me a new dog. A German shepherd! For my twelfth birthday, my dad and I went into town and bought a puppy at the animal market, a cross between a German shepherd and a Caucasian shepherd dog. The puppy was tiny, just over a week old. He could barely crawl and he barely ate, and he fit easily on my childish palm; he had no breed registration documents, but he cost only fifteen rubles. At night, he squealed and crawled all over my bedroom floor, until my mum had had enough and came and put him in my bed, where he warmed himself up and fell asleep. At first, I fed the puppy by dipping my finger in milk and sticking it in his mouth, as he still hadn't learned to lap it up. We called the little guy Dick.

The dog grew quickly. He was strong, shaggy, and clumsy and, like all puppies, loved to play. When Dick grew up, I was a bit disappointed: a mongrel is a mongrel, and, although they do cross German shepherds with Caucasians to try and get the best of both breeds, my dog didn't look like any of the pictures in the little book on dogs that this old guy I knew had once let me borrow. For a while it really bothered me, but eventually my love for the dog overcame my awareness of his imperfections.

My dog grew up big and strong. His reddish-black coat made him look more like a German shepherd, but his big bones were unmistakably Caucasian, as were his ears, which drooped at the ends, and his slightly curly tail. Dick grew very attached to me, and I to him. We walked a lot, and I trained him—he learned to do some of the things that a working dog should be able to do. Although, at the same time, he had a rather wayward character. His hunting instinct would always come through whenever he saw

13

a chicken, a duck, or similar prey, which led to innumerable conflicts with the owners of such ravaged beasts, including with my own parents.

I usually took Dick to the forest that grew near our village, on the other side of the field, up the hill. We would walk alone, or sometimes with my friends, who brought their own dogs, though none of them was as beautiful as mine. It was fun to hang out in a gang, but I preferred walking alone in the forest with my dog. They were unforgettable moments. When he searches for you, after you've deliberately stayed behind a bit and hidden in the bushes. Searches for you and finds you. And how happy you are when you find each other again after such a brief parting. The dog is happy that he found his master, and the master is happy that he has such a clever dog, and you're both happy because you love each other and you're together again. Or how exciting it is when you come across a hare that sits quietly until the last moment and then shoots away from under your very feet, and you watch your seemingly unwieldy dog suddenly turn into an arrow, flattening his ears, and, squealing a bit, rush after the animal, gradually losing ground.

How beautiful it is to walk on a damp autumn day, in

the long, bright twilight, when there's nobody around, it smells of rotting wood, and there's a light haze in the air.

Winter is also good for walking, when snow, so rare in our parts, falls, and you see footprints, your own and those of others, when your voice rings out and carries itself far into the distance, when you shout with all your might: "Dick, come here!" and then you hear the beating of his paws, followed by his breathing, and then you see your dog running toward you, knocking snow onto himself from the low-hanging branches. And on a summer evening, how wonderful it is to return from a walk when the air is full of sound, and it smells of a downpour that hasn't yet happened, and when you come out of the forest you suddenly become aware that the whisper of the leaves is much too loud, and you realize that it's raining, that it has started and is following you through the forest. And you start running as fast as you can down through the field, and your dog runs with you, turning his head toward you, and halfway home the rain catches you. And then you walk home together, and you take him on his leash, and all the dogs on the street go crazy, and yours answers with his own thunderous bark, and you can barely hold him back, and you are both tired and happy. Then you give him some water, you pour it from the jug into his bowl, and then you bring him his supper. You both fall asleep happy. And next morning you go to school, and the dog, dragging his chain, follows you to the gate, and you both know that in the evening there'll be another walk, and you'll be together again, and you'll be happy again.

Childhood is a happy time. Thank God I had a happy childhood, in which the warmest and most cherished moments are those spent walking my dog.

But then childhood gradually finished, and walking the dog turned into a tiresome obligation, or an excuse to go and have a smoke or play cards with the guys in the forest. In summer, I dedicated more evenings to my friends and to football than to walking my dog. And every time he saw me approaching the gates, Dick would jump out of his kennel with hope in his eyes that we would go for a walk, but almost every time he was disappointed. At first, I always stopped, stroked him, and apologized that we wouldn't be going for a walk that day, and he would lick my face, and we'd part. Later, I would give him a quick pat on the head before going out, and later still I would just walk right past him. The further I progressed through school, the rarer our walks became, the less time I dedicated to my dog, and soon the walks stopped entirely. I found new interests, new friends, and the dog faded into the background, like a wife that you continue to live with but stop noticing.

Later, when I'd finished school, I went to study in the city and only saw Dick once a week. I would stroke him when I arrived, sometimes when I was leaving. Did I still love him? Of course I did, but that love had already turned into a habit, like the way you love old people. Dick was already ten years old by then, and he'd started to age. Did he still love me the way he had before? I think so. It was my mum who looked after him in those later years—fed him and let him out for the night into the yard or the street—but a dog chooses only one master and stays faithful to him until the end. Dick started to get sick, then his back legs started to buckle under him; he'd rarely get up; he had rheumatism. I had suffered from this illness myself as a child, and my family knew how to fight it. We started to inject him with the necessary medicine. Dick improved, gained strength, and he managed to keep going for another year and a half.

He died a long and painful death. While we were trying to decide whether to put him to sleep or not, it all finished. I came back from the city, put him in a large crate and dragged him off on a metal trolley to bury him. In his old age, Dick had dried up and shrunk to about half his original size, but all the same he was pretty heavy.

I buried him myself on a vacant lot that was slowly turning into a rubbish dump, next to the road that leads to the forest, the same one we used to like to walk along. I dug a hole, put the dog in it, and began to bury him. I had nothing to cover him with, and, after my first spadeful of earth landed on the dog's muzzle, I stopped. It was hard. I couldn't do it. After the second spadeful, tears welled up in my eyes. When the earth closed up over the dog, then it got easier. I would never have thought it would be harder to bury my dog than my father.

•

They say there's no such thing as bad people, only bad deeds. That's true. There is at least a bit of goodness in every person. It's called kindness. And the kinder a person is, the better he is. All our kindness is instilled in us in childhood. It's the gentleness of our mothers and the hands of our fathers, it's our friends, it's fairy tales and books. It's the cartoons we watch. In the little mammoth swimming toward his mum in the ice floe there's more kindness than in all the charitable organizations put together! And kindness is also love. And not only love for your parents, for your kith and kin, but also for animals. Especially domestic animals, especially your pets.

And the best thing of all is to love a dog, and to have the dog love you. Cats and especially parrots—they are incapable of love. They're capable of living, but not of loving. Love for a dog is the closest thing there is to love for a woman. Your mum can love you, but she also has to love your dad, your brothers and sisters, her own mother and father, and maybe also your neighbor, Uncle Petya, though that's none of our business . . . But a dog will love only you and will be devoted only to you. And it asks for nothing in return. Apart from your love.

Childhood

Everybody says childhood is the happiest time in your life. Agreed. But I would also add that it is the brightest. Usually. For almost everybody. I feel truly sorry for all those who never had a childhood, or for whom it finished early, or for whom it wasn't bright enough.

I had it all: a childhood, and enough light in it. And that light can't be measured in terms of two kilograms of mandarins at New Year or cartoons on the black-and-white television. Nor can it be measured in birthday presents.

When you're eight, a set of Hungarian plastic soldiers is the limit of your ambitions. A radio-controlled car is nothing but a sweet dream. But whether you had soldiers or a car, after enough years have passed it no longer means anything. And as an adult you understand that all this stuff gathering dust in the attic isn't important at all. But you also understand that back there, in your childhood, for you, as a child, it wasn't really the main thing either.

The main thing—what was and should be the main thing—is your mum, your family, it's your friends, it's your beloved animals, everything alive that surrounds you, that gives you light that will make you glow from the inside, forever, so that there will be no such thing as "after." After childhood.

•

I remember myself as a really young child. Sometimes I even think I can remember faces leaning over me as I lay in my crib (although now I'm inclined to think that this is just a scene from a film that stuck in my mind).

I was aware of myself as an individual very early too, when I was about five. I got a splinter in my finger and couldn't pull it out. Some friend, for some reason I really can't remember who that little shit was, told me that that was it, the end, the splinter would travel from my finger to my heart and I would die.

This is my first clear impression from my childhood: I'm five years old, I'm on my way home from kindergarten, wearing sandals and shorts, walking up a small hill near our village (for some reason kids don't like roads, they're always taking short cuts, and if the road is straight, they'll go crawling off around the bushes). So, I'm up high, the whole village spread out below me, the kindergarten behind me, far off to the left is the school that I still haven't been in, and in my mind I'm saying goodbye to all this, getting ready to die. The scene is calm, moderately tragic, windy. But I'm not crying. If that's how it is to be, that's how it'll be.

I can't remember what happened next, these early childhood memories are only fragments, but, given that I'm still alive, the splinter must have missed my heart.

•

I'm six. On the street, it's almost evening, we're playing soldiers. I've got my machine gun and my friend with me, we're hiding behind a rock near my house. Suddenly, someone sneaks up from behind, pulls the plastic pistol from behind my belt and sticks it into my back. I turn around—my dad. "Dad, don't get in the way!" His strong, calloused driver's hands, black with bloody smudges from doing repairs. He's on his way home from work. Sober. I'm happy.

•

It's surprising which fragments memory preserves from childhood. I'm seven. My mum is beating my bare legs with a
rubber tube—the neighbor's daughters told her that I was
throwing stones and broke their window. It wasn't me, I was
just standing watching as some of the other kids threw stones
at them, and a lot of windows were broken that day—in the
quarry near our houses they'd overdone it with the dynamite.
But it was me that got beaten with the tube. It was really painful. But even worse—it was unfair. For nothing . . . I wasn't
beaten often, only a few times, and each time for the deeds
of others.

By the way, about the quarry! What, you didn't grow
up right next to a stone quarry? Strange. I did. Very close by.
And there were regular explosions, every day at lunchtime.
The siren was always unexpected—twice, once long and
once short. Then, after a pause—the explosion. If you managed to run outside in time and guessed correctly where to
look you could catch sight of a small cloud of dust up on
the hill.

•

Eight years old. As always, my friends came round in the morning, we collected a whole jar full of Colorado beetles and built a prison camp for them out of sand and bits of rubbish . . .

It was my birthday party that evening. Lots of guests, my parents' friends. They give me presents, mostly money—such big, important-looking bits of paper, red or blue with Lenin's portrait in profile. It feels kind of nice, exciting, like I'm being treated like an adult. The next morning you'll give them to your mum. She won't even ask for them, you'll give them yourself, as you should. Then she'll buy you something with them or they'll go toward the family's needs, to top up the family budget after the cost of the party—you have to give your aunts and uncles plenty to eat and drink. And you're left with this feeling of emptiness, of having been tricked. And after that I didn't like getting the bits of paper with Lenin's profile on them for my birthday.

Now, if someone shows up to my child's birthday with money instead of a present, well, I don't envy him. I can scare myself sometimes.

Money doesn't mean anything to a child. In my first year of school I found a ruble and a half on the sports field. I didn't know what to do with it. It was the same feeling as if today I were to find a million dollar note with a special mark for ultraviolent lamps saying "Approved by the Economic Crime Commission"—so much money and nowhere to go. At that time, I was getting ten kopecks a day for lunch, enough for a large jam bun (which never seemed to have any jam in it). And here was a ruble and a half. Not knowing what to do with it and not wanting to tell my parents, I hid the money somewhere, and then later couldn't find it again, and I felt better—more money more problems, a weight off the shoulders, and so on . . .

•

Nine. We bought a car. An old Moskvich. We started taking occasional trips to the sea—not in the murderously suffocating, slow bus, not sitting on wooden benches on the open back of one of the kolkhoz's Gazik trucks, but in our own car! I didn't think it was cool—there was no such thing as cool back then—it was just comfortable and fast. The best part about visiting the sea is trying to pick out its thin line, a slightly different color from the blue sky, far off in the distance: when the car reaches the crest of the last hill and you finally see it, that thin line at the edge of the sky, the sea! You'll be there soon. But you're happy already.

•

Ten. The street by my house, evening, dusk. We're playing hide-and-seek. Boys and girls. It's almost dark already. A little longer and you won't be able to see a thing. But there's still time to play, just a little longer. You just really want to keep playing, as long as possible. Everyone together, completely absorbed in the game, having fun. I'm running past my gate, and I can smell fried potatoes coming from our summer kitchen—soon I'll be called to eat. I'll hear the opening music of the nightly episode of the spy drama coming through the open window of our house, and after supper I'll just have time to catch the end.

This is the image that has stayed most clearly in my memory from childhood. I close my eyes and I can still see it—the street, the dusk, the game, the smell of potatoes, and the sound of the TV. I want to freeze that moment and live in it for eternity. Although really, I guess that moment already is eternity for me.

If you never spent even one summer in the countryside,

if you never played hide-and-seek with your friends at dusk, then you never had the childhood that all children deserve.

•

Eleven. Our street: Makar, Sanya, Taksik, and I have finalized our unification with the kids from the next street: Lelya, Barsuk, Oleg, and Belan.

Summer. We're playing chizh on the road: you take turns throwing long sticks to knock over two cans piled one on top of one the other; you then gather up your sticks, and whoever managed to win the first stage now has to protect the cans (the chizh), now piled on top of each other again, which involves fending off the other players with a stick as they try to knock them over. Getting hit on the fingers with a stick is a distinct childhood sensation.

Lelya is the ringleader, he's about five years older than me, almost an adult, always dressed in sports pants and a white vest, always joking and teasing us, and we let him.

Makar is big and fat, my neighbor, one of those friends from the playground who usually wouldn't stick in your memory, four years older than me. Makar is my close friend, so nobody bothers me.

Sanya and Taksik are in the same class in school, a year older than me, they live three doors down on my street, on opposite sides.

Barsuk is the only one who's younger than me, but he's Lelya's neighbor, so nobody bothers him either, except Lelya himself, but he bothers everybody.

Oleg has learning difficulties, an outsize moron, also a lot older than me, he's well-adjusted and violent only sometimes.

Belan and Sanya are from good families—the local intelligentsia, the village elites.

We were a cheerful bunch, or, as they say now but didn't say then—a gang. In school we barely spoke to one another, since we were in different classes, but we spent almost all our free time together.

•

When I was twelve, I got a bike, like almost everyone else in our gang, and then it started: raids on the strawberry fields and orchards, getting chased by guards, long distance rides on the roads and off-road, including water obstacles, regular races for bets, etc., etc. . . . Constantly falling off, the grazes on our elbows and knees never managing to completely heal . . . And why did Sanya and I decide to have a bet about who could ride farther—no hands, no brakes—down that (seemingly) not-too-steep hill? Sanya lost, braking in front of a flock of geese, and I was rewarded with a scar on my left cheek that didn't disappear for several years; the goose got a dislocated wing, and my mum a mild heart attack when they dragged me home. In short, nobody came out of it well . . . But it was impossible to live without all this.

•

Thirteen was the height of my football obsession. We had been playing for a few years—in spring, autumn, a bit in winter, but you couldn't beat summer for football! Two football fields were built on patches of open ground, and we played against other streets. Victories and defeats. Fights after the games—one on one, everyone watching, nobody intervening.

Almost every day, when the heat has dropped and you've done everything you can to help your family around the house, you listen and wait for that sound—have they started kicking the ball around on the next street? That means we'll be playing at home. Or if I can hear the measured sound of a ball striking the asphalt, that means Lelya has come out and is bouncing the ball with all his strength as he walks from his street to ours, and that means we're getting a whole crowd together and heading off to play somewhere else! Time to get changed fast! Socks on, quick! I sit on the porch and lace up my football trainers. I do it quickly, but carefully, so I won't have to retie them later. Time goes slowly. Very slowly. A minute spent tying laces seems like an hour. The tension becomes unbearable. The last knot—and I'm ready! I cover the ten meters to the gate like a bullet, not always managing to pet my dog, who doesn't always manage to run out in time to catch me, and I leap out into the street. Our gang is all there. Football! The game won't start for a while, but the boring ritual of lacing up my trainers is done. A hot summer's day, in which nothing remarkable happened, is behind me. Now there will be football. And I'll be playing. With all the others. Until evening. Until it's dark. Until our shirts are sweaty and our legs are aching. Until we're grazed and blistered, we'll play. God, how good it is! Thank you for making it happen!

•

Fourteen. Childhood was beginning to end. Slowly but surely and irreversibly. My friends joined the army, went to study in the city, or pursued some other interests, and our company fell apart.

When I was small, I thought that the world was limited to what I could see with my own eyes. In other words, my world was defined by the horizon. We lived in an area of foothills, so the horizon wasn't too far away: there was raised ground all around. The world around me was like a large bowl, lined at the edges by mountains, hills, and fields. The world for me had limits, but it wasn't limited. It was full, a full cup of childhood happiness. When I was small, I thought that when the sun set in the evening it hid itself in a big net stuck to the back wall of the mountain, just like the elasticized nets attached to the walls of third-class railway carriages for you to keep your stuff in. And behind the mountain there's nothing—I can't see anything there, so there can't be anything there. And the sun had its own nighttime life, in that net it had a few little sun-children, a little sun family, and it was neither boring nor too crowded in there. I don't remember the moment when I understood that there was no such net, that the world continued beyond the mountain. And I don't remember when that cup of my childhood world stopped existing. Just stopped, and that was it. All that remained was light, light from childhood.

•

Fifteen years have passed. I've lived in the city for a long time and I rarely visit the village.

Makar went off the rails: he drank for years and then came back, joining the ranks of the semi-homeless village alcoholics.

Sanya moved to another city and also rarely comes home.

Taksik, like all four of us from our street, lost his father, but he wasn't finished off by some illness caused by drinking—he hanged himself. Because of the drinking. By that time his brother had already been shot, so it was hardly surprising that Taksik and his mum are now ardent members of a religious sect.

Lelya came home, got married, got fat, but is still a joker.

Oleg, like Makar, hit the bottle hard. The bottle doesn't care if you're smart or stupid, it drowns everyone.

Barsuk narrowly avoided jail, so he's still around, he borrowed some money from me at some point.

Belan drives a truck.

Childhood is finished, it doesn't live in those places anymore. The places are the same and the people are supposedly the same, but everything is different.

•

When we're children we do everything at top speed, we never have enough time, we're always in a rush, everything is interesting, we have to go everywhere—we have plenty of energy but no time. Everything is too slow, everything drags on too long. School never ends. Ten years feels like nothing compared to that bell that will never ring!

The boy hopping on one leg trying to catch up with his cycling grandfather couldn't care less how he looks to others—he's in a hurry, he's running, his heart is bursting. I don't want to be slow. I don't want to rush. I never want to think about how I look to others. I want to feel like I'm my heart is bursting. Maybe childhood has finished, but I'm still going to hop along on one leg.

Hospital

Anyone who was lucky enough to be born in the USSR, and, come to think of it, anyone who wasn't lucky enough to be born in that country but was born all the same, should have, at least once in their lives, and maybe even more than once, spent some time in a hospital. I've only been in kids' hospitals, I've avoided adult ones, but I don't imagine they are very different. In my early childhood, before I got sick, I was rarely in the hospital, only once. After I got sick, I was there all the time.

A six-year-old boy hit his armpit on the back of a chair while jumping off a table (it's not clear why he did it, but it was clearly very important for him), and he got a lump under there, quite a big one. It didn't hurt, but it bothered him when he moved his arm and, when it grew to the size of a walnut, it began to worry both the boy and his mother.

When, after a month, all the old wives' lotions and spells had failed, they resorted to extreme measures in the shape of a surgical ward and all that they do there.

He doesn't remember the doctor shouting at his mother, he only remembers the oxygen mask, like a pilot's, over his face and the words, "Now we're going to fly." Two weeks later the boy was walking around the hospital corridors, a chessboard under his healthy arm, looking for his next victim, someone he hadn't yet harassed and defeated. I'm told that I was that boy.

•

It would take an entire book to enumerate all my childhood cuts, grazes, scratches, and bruises (things that were called "boo-boos" back then), and any man worth his salt could fill a hundred pages or more with his childhood injuries, but it would interest nobody, least of all me. This is all just normal stuff for a normal boy. So it was for me, until I got sick, and I stopped being normal and became unwell.

Before that, I hadn't understood that stupid toast, "To your health!" When I was young I didn't understand it at all, though when I had children I at least understood the toast "To the children's health!" Because you know that they are the most important thing you have and that health is the most important thing they have. And you don't have to drink yourself stupid toasting this every night, but you do have to always look after your health and always remember about it. Every day, and often even at night too.

When you're a child you don't understand why your mum yelled at you so much when the neighbors' kid got back to your house faster than you could and shouted, "Auntie Liusya, your son crashed!" And he got there faster than you because you can't even walk, never mind run, and you're trying not to look at your messed up leg, and your bike, which you'll somehow need to drag home, is in an even worse state, and for the moment you don't even feel pain, just the damp sock on your leg . . .

•

That teacher lady wasn't to blame. After all, she couldn't know that she'd get stuck in the shops for three hours, and winter wasn't really so harsh that year, and the children on the excursion, when there's enough of them, will always find something to do outside—there are trees, pavement, cars driving around—plenty of excitement. So they got a bit cold—it happens to everyone, and they didn't all get sick, after all, did they? I got a cold after that school trip. A normal cold, nothing special, I got better quickly. I went to school on Monday, fifth grade, you have to work hard, can't afford to miss anything. Except my legs wouldn't straighten completely—it was curious, a bit uncomfortable, but I didn't want my parents to notice.

On Tuesday the boy got worse again—let him stay in bed. Says he's got pains in his legs, it's probably the weather . . . The boy stayed home alone, but he could no longer get up. It's a good thing his father came home at lunch time and calmly carried the boy to the car and took him to the hospital. There, also calmly, they informed them that it was good he hadn't brought him on Wednesday, otherwise he'd have been in a wheelchair to the end of his days.

•

And you reckon you can't get rheumatism, polyarthritis, and myocarditis all in one go at the age of eleven? Look after your colds, and don't push your luck.

About six weeks in bed, another six weeks of your usual

routine, and then you're almost free, you can go off to a sanatorium for six months if you like. And the boy went. And then he went again, and then again. Sometimes you end up paying a lot for small mistakes, especially if they have to do with children's health.

•

It was always fun in the sanatoriums—that small, communal, and relatively independent children's world. A little, soft school of life. But I have neither the space nor the desire to talk a lot about it. The most interesting part was running after the waves. The sanatorium was on the beach. The beach was sandy with a gentle slope, and the breakers were long, and in a storm even longer, maybe ten or fifteen meters, and near the building there was a small wooden pier on stilts. During storms, we used to run alongside the pier toward the sea behind the retreating waves, and, at the last minute, grab the pier railings and pull up our legs. The wave would rush back in underneath you toward the shore, roaring and spitting, and you hung on, waiting for the wave to roll back out and expose the beach again, then you would leap off and run back, with the next wave chasing hard on your heels. I never had more fun with anything in my child-hood than with those waves! If you were bold and got lucky with the wave, you could get to the very end of the pier and hang there for a long time, waiting for the right moment to return. If you weren't so bold, if you hesitated or just weren't lucky—whether with the wave or with your parents show-ing up—then you'd end up going back home, that is, to the sanatorium, to get changed. At the sanatorium there was another great adolescent-erotic game—climbing between the balconies on the fourth floor into the girls' rooms. You could hang out with them during the day, of course, but nighttime was something entirely different. And even if the girls were nothing special and you didn't even notice them during the day, at night, when you got into their rooms (they always let you in, at any time, into any room— they, it seems, had their own, female game—waiting), everything was dif-ferent, more interesting, more exciting . . . in other words, the standard beginnings of the process of sexual maturation.

•

I guess different people have different experiences of sanato-riums in this life, but mine were full of excitement. Except that's not what I wanted to talk about. I wanted to talk about a certain hospital. The last children's hospital in my life, or rather, in my childhood.

A typical regional hospital, entirely satisfactory—good people, good doctors doing serious operations, saving kids, doing all kinds of treatments. And there's one operation they do there that, if it's really necessary and unavoidable, then you really have to do it, otherwise things will be bad, you can spend the rest of your life speaking through your nose and with your mouth hanging open. I'm talking about a tonsillectomy. Among the simple folk, to whom I belong and from whom I would never separate myself, we called it "having your glands out." So if you or your kids are ever told that you or they need a tonsillectomy, don't believe it: they're going to take your glands out!

I had the operation pretty late—I was almost fourteen, but I was still a sickly kid and got angina and colds all the time, so my mum agreed. Jumping forward I have to admit, the operation helped. I got sick less often, and, when a couple of years later I decided to ignore all medicine and its bans on physical exertion, I almost stopped getting sick. Rheumatism forgot all about me then, and my children's medical card (I don't even have an adult one) was soon gathering dust in a drawer. Every so often I get it out and use it to frighten particularly sensitive pediatricians when I go to get my kids checked up.

•

Tonsillectomy. I don't know how the Cheka used to torture its enemies, but if that's how the Soviet Union did operations on their kids, then I'm not surprised that the Red Terror triumphed over the Whites.

They don't feed you all morning, so you don't puke all over the staff. Then they dress you up in a gown, put a sort of hood made of two bits of cloth on your head, with a small opening for your mouth, and send you off to languish in the waiting room. If I had the same terrible sense of humor then that I do now, I'd definitely have said, "Guys, looks they're going to shoot us in the mouth!" There's still room for joking at that moment, though the background racket made up of frequent children's screams from behind the door might instill a certain feeling of trepidation.

Then they lead the little dummies with nappies on their heads one by one into the torture chamber. Why did I have to look from underneath my veil at the range of medical instruments on the table? None of them looked like it'd be particularly beneficial for my health. Then they strap all the movable parts of your body, including your head, to the chair with belts. "What is this, electrotherapy? Don't overdo it with the voltage!" the hero of an American comedy would joke. But I wasn't laughing. I had the distinct feeling that things were about to get extremely unfunny.

What they were doing inside my mouth, I can't tell—I didn't see it, and I don't want to imagine it. Only once, briefly, when I somehow managed to move my head and could see through the opening for my mouth with one eye, I saw a girl of about ten years old in the next chair . . . I was glad I was a boy, strong and brave, and being held down by only two nurses instead of by the whole department.

After finishing with my tonsils, the quacks unexpectedly discovered I had enlarged adenoids. After a short and whispered discussion, the question was posed to the victim: "Shall we take them out now? Or would you like to come back to us later?" They may have understood that I'd hardly be in a rush to come back, or interpreted my stamping my feet and moaning as an affirmative reply; either way, the doctor pulled out a hook so enormous that I managed to see it even through the nappy, and I realized this was the last thing I would ever see, and so I should do my best to fix it in my memory. I hadn't thought that my adenoids would be stuck inside my skull somewhere in the region of the crown of my head—though really, how could I have thought anything at all at that moment, given that my brain had retreated into my scrotum at the beginning of the operation and hadn't even dared to peek out from there? But that's where the doctor found them. The adenoids put up a short but extremely fierce fight.

I had heard that novocaine was a good painkiller, but during my operation I felt like it wasn't helping me at all. How wrong I was. When they took me to the ward and laid me on a bed—after this transformative operation almost nobody is able to move around independently—I decided that everything was behind me now: the pain would subside and I'd start to feel better. But that's not how it went. Novocaine is a good painkiller after all, but it has one drawback—it doesn't last forever. An hour later the pain was such that I was beating the wall with all my limbs: it felt like I had ten of those limbs, all throbbing at once, like a grenade was exploding in my head on a loop, and like the place where they'd ripped my throat apart was on fire, and it felt like all this went on for a year or maybe two.

It seems that, at some point during those nightmarish lunchtime hours, my organism took the decision, at the very basic cellular level, never to have recourse to free Soviet medical provision again, or from any other medical provision for that matter. My brain certainly took no part in making this decision, being busy making the tortuous journey from the region of my sexual organs back into the temporarily vacated brain cavity.

•

After lunch, my friend from the neighboring ward visited (people usually find each other quickly in hospitals) and brought me half of a huge watermelon. I don't really like watermelon much on a good day, and at that moment I really didn't feel like it. I couldn't say this—for a few days after that I could barely swallow, never mind speak—but my friend read it on my face and made a retreat before I could start thumping the walls.

In the next bed, having exactly the same convulsions, was a boy with Down syndrome, two or three years younger than me. That same day, they'd done to him what they'd done to me. Now I know he had Down syndrome, but then we just thought he was a bit slow, a bit dumb. The third boy in our ward was from a good family, but he hadn't had an operation, he was getting treated for something else, but I didn't see him that day, he had managed to slip out somehow and appeared only in the evening, when the whole catastrophe was over.

•

That was one of the worst days of my life, but not because of the operation or the pain after it. I'd have gone through it all again, if only what happened later hadn't happened. Although maybe it had to be that way. I don't know.

As I already said, it ended up being a terrible day, but initially it had been a beautiful day. I still didn't know what awaited me, it was my second day in the hospital, I already knew everybody, everybody knew me, I was one of the older ones, the cool ones, not like the rest of the small fry. All morning my new friend and I were having fun around the hospital. In our ward, the kid from the good family was making fun of the kid with Down's, the slow one. No, he didn't beat him or call him names, he was just screwing with him, as they say. The boy from the good family was mocking the kid with Down's by pretending to throw his sock out of the window while actually hiding it inside his closed fist, and then revealing the sock again. The smart kid was fooling the not-so-smart one. A few demonstrations like this were enough to convince the kid with Down's that the window was magical, and so he started chucking his own stuff through it—socks, underpants, some other belongings. It flew out of the fifth-floor window and none of it came flying back. The not-so-smart kid couldn't understand what was wrong and kept throwing his clothes out of the window until there was nothing left. Whether he just didn't have many clothes or had eventually understood that the trick wasn't working, he stopped and returned to his bed.

All that time the boy from the good family was laughing his head off in his bed, egging on the kid with Down's in between fits of laughter. I lay in my bed with my book and observed all this in silence, maybe laughing a bit myself at all this mockery. I was older than both of them and could have stopped this at any time, but I didn't stop it. I didn't like what was going on, maybe everything was just happening too quickly and unpredictably, I'd never encountered a kid with mental problems before, maybe it was because I'd been an outcast myself until recently and wanted to look at this from the outside too, I don't know, I don't remember. The thing is, I could have stopped it, but I didn't.

•

After our afternoon nap the nurse came and asked where the not-so-smart kid's clothes were. The boy from the good family said that the slow kid had thrown them out the window himself, and technically speaking he was right. And here I also kept quiet, I couldn't turn him in, it wouldn't be cool, and we could both get a clip round the ear for mistreating a disabled child. And the kid just pointed at the window and mumbled something only he could understand, he couldn't really talk so well.

But that was yesterday, and yesterday was a good day, and by the evening the incident had been forgotten—some of his stuff had been brought back, some had gotten lost, but before evening so many things happened that the episode with the window was erased from memory.

•

And today, today was like my worst nightmare and then some: I thought they were going to permanently mutilate me in the morning, then that I was going to kick the bucket at lunchtime. At least in the evening the pain got a little bit better.

That evening, after lights out, the kid with Down's got a visit from his mum. Turns out that slow kids have mums, and they love their kids, and their kids love them. She came to see him after the operation and he laid his head on her lap, curled up like a little dog, and she stroked him. And I felt ashamed, so unbelievably ashamed, because of what happened the previous day, I wanted to jump out of bed and give the boy from the good family a good kicking and apologize to the mum of the kid with Down's—not to him, he wouldn't have understood anyway, but to her. Why did she come so late? Maybe she was working late, or lives far away, but she still came. Doesn't seem like the dad is on the scene: surely they would have come together, it's late after all, and the boy just had an operation; or maybe he just doesn't want anything to do with the kid—some dads don't want anything to do even with normal kids. And she came alone and late, and her kid curls up on her lap, and he'll never be normal, and she knows it, but she loves him, you can tell. But I don't get up, and don't apologize, and don't beat up the other boy—it was too late now, I should have done something yesterday, but so I just lie there saying nothing, scared to move during that whole silent meeting of mother and son.

•

Next day, I felt better, the pain was passing. I drank some thin warm soup, it was painful to swallow and speak. The boy from the good family also got a visit from his mum, and again I had the chance to witness it. But I didn't like this kid anymore, and that feeling spread to his mum, and to his dad, who, by the way, also didn't appear, but somehow you felt that he was around.

And again, I said nothing, but it would have been pointless to say anything anyway.

•

The next day we started flying paper planes. I say paper, because now you can get all kinds of beautiful plastic models and toy planes that really fly, but then there were only paper planes. We made them by tearing up a school exercise book and making ninety six separate sheets of paper, so we ended up with almost one hundred little white planes all covered in the thin squares of exercise paper. The whole of nap time we spent folding them, and then, after our afternoon snack, we launched them from the balcony. It was really beautiful—some were still in the air, some already landed, but we kept launching them . . .

"We" were my friend, another two kids from our ward, and me. To make the story more poetic I could say that the kid with Down's and the boy from the good family were with us too, but they weren't. Nobody wanted to have to look after the simple kid, and the good kid turned out to be not so good in pretty much every respect, even without taking into account the incident with the window, which nobody but me knew about. And boys are pretty strict about this kind of thing—if you're a little shit, you'll lose your friends pretty quick.

•

For me, this last stay in the kids' hospital feels like a very distinct moment in my life, the moment when my childhood ended. The process of maturing—finishing childhood, becoming an adult, getting old, and less noticeable changes—does not happen according to a calendar, nor is it smooth and unnoticed, but rather it happens in stages, when something in a person builds up, ripens, and then something happens and a person is transformed, in a day or two or a week, and he's suddenly jumped over some line, suddenly something clicks, and you're already on to the next stage, and you're already different, and then another year, two, or three of internal, not entirely conscious preparation, and another click, and another stage . . .

After that hospital I was more grown up, I was a bit different, I had almost said goodbye to childhood. I don't know what had a greater impact on me, the pain or my guilty conscience because I hadn't stood up for the boy, or maybe the one hundred paper planes. I don't know, but something clicked inside.

What exactly clicked? That doesn't matter. What matters is that since then I've never kept quiet when I saw somebody trying to humiliate someone else, and I know that I never will.

School

At our party for finishing kindergarten I wasn't given a schoolbag. Everybody lined up and got one, but I didn't. My mum was a teacher in the kindergarten, and she took me to one side and told me I'd get a schoolbag later, not the same kind as everyone else got, but better. And they really did give it to me later. It was a kind of dark blue color, not brown like all the others. It was nicer, with straps, a real satchel, not one of those simple brown bags with only a handle. I guess I was meant to be happy about it, but I wasn't. I didn't want a special schoolbag, I wanted a normal one, like everyone else had, and I wanted to get it when everyone else got theirs, and not on my own, as though it were a secret.

But I did want to go to school. Even though most of the kids didn't want to go, and it was even kind of cool to say "no" when adults asked you if you were looking forward to going to school. That was considered normal, adults didn't tell you off for it, they just patted you on the back and said never mind, you'll grow to like it. But my answer was, "Yes, I do want to go to school." So they didn't pat me on the back and had nothing to say to me.

All my life I wanted to be like everyone else, but somehow I could never manage it. I was always alone, on the sidelines.

I got to ring the first bell of the school year. I hadn't been expecting it, nobody warned me, although the adults had probably decided beforehand. Now I understand that there just weren't—and couldn't be—any other candidates: I was the smartest boy in the group, my mum was a teacher in our kindergarten, and I had a special, sort of dark blue satchel. I was led out by a girl from one of the senior classes, probably an A-grade student, and I rang the bell. Or rather, I tried to. The bell rang really badly: it had a metal nut on a string inside it that was meant to make the noise, but since I was elegantly holding the bell by its handle, with the actual bell part pointing upwards, the nut had fallen somewhere inside and had gotten stuck on something, so the bell refused to ring. The A grader and I walked around the playground—I was a dazed little kid, tired out, like all the other new first graders, from standing in sunbaked lines all day—and I tried, with a stupid grin on my face, to ring the unringable bell. Eventually I started shaking it harder, and the nut managed to produce a few miserable, tinny chimes as we made our way to the high stairway leading to the school. Then they started playing some kind of school waltz over the speakers and we all went up into the land of weighty knowledge.

I liked school, but not for long. I liked studying, but not necessarily going to school. The Soviet education system broke me down with its routine, its rote learning, its ponderous lessons as thick as tar. I liked gym class, woodwork and metalwork, and the breaks, where you at least had some kind of freedom. I can't say I liked math—liking math seems a bit abnormal to me, like being a kid and dreaming of working as a cashier—but I found it pretty easy, and finished all the class tests in half the time allowed. Russian language classes were really boring, but I really loved literature and history, those lessons were way more interesting and somehow also a bit freer than the others. The Russian and literature teachers always read my essays aloud, standing in the middle of the classroom, which impressed nobody, least of all me.

In just a few years in the Pioneers, I managed to make the meteoric rise from head of class to bugler. It was clear almost right away that I had no special desire to be civically or politically active, and nobody else in the class could play the bugle, or, at least, I could play better than anyone else .. . And right until my final days in the Pioneers I played the same simple little melody at all ceremonial events, all the carryings in and carryings out of the banners and similar nonsense, standing beside the drummer, again, somewhere on the sidelines.

The village teachers were pretty bad, but they were mostly kind: bad people don't go to work in schools. But it's only now I understand that the level of teaching wasn't up to much. Then, from the third row, it all seemed pretty impressive. But one time a Russian teacher from the city spent a year at our school. Somehow, she hadn't managed to get a job for that school year, and so she came out every day to our village to teach the local dunces, including me. I couldn't tell, sitting in fifth grade, that she was a really good, talented teacher, I just knew her classes were really interesting, even the Russian language classes, never mind literature, which at that point became not only my favorite lesson, but my favorite subject of all. She opened up a whole new world for me—how, by what means, I don't remember, but after a year of her teaching something changed inside me. She was a real teacher. And then after a year she went back to the city and we got another teacher, one who used to teach the youngest classes but had done some distance study with the pedagogical institute and decided she should move up to training the older pupils. And for the first time I started to have conflicts with a teacher—I was amazed how different they were in their approaches, and by the new teacher's stupid demands and blind routines. Now you could read only recommended chapters, instead of whole books. How can you read just some chapters of a book? What could you possibly understand from it? Just to be able to answer the questions at the end of the textbook? This really annoyed me, and I didn't stay quiet about it. I thought it was really boring, but I was only thirteen, had no arguments to put forward, and could do nothing more than turn my irritation into rows with the teacher. The rest of the class, all those A-grade girls and B-grade boys who knew the school program inside out and wrote in nice, neat handwriting in their neat exercise books, couldn't care less. The rest, those who lived according to the principle of "please don't ask me," were also unconcerned with such problems: for them, it wasn't even a problem. But I kept asking difficult questions and was rewarded by repeatedly being sent out of the class. I spent half of my literature and history classes in the corridor.

History became my second-favorite subject. The history teacher was a lot more intelligent that the hysterical Russian teacher, though she also didn't like constantly having to deal with awkward questions, which were a matter of princi-ple for me and which I asked with an unrestrained youth-ful zeal and a complete lack of tolerance, and so I got sent into the corridor here too. From the window of the cor-ridor near the Russian classroom you could see the main school entrance, where there would always be somebody doing something, so it wasn't too boring, and from the cor-ridor near the history classroom you had a great view of the school playing fields, and you could often see kids running around in brightly colored sports outfits, while those who'd been excused from physical exercise but still had to attend the lessons sat on benches, all wearing the identical brown uniforms of the schoolchildren of the country of slaves.

But I have to give credit to both my teachers—they didn't lower my grades, though I imagine that even today they would both probably start shaking at the mention of my name.

When I was a child, I was friends with Misha. When I

was a child, I had a lot of friends, and Misha and I were in the same group in kindergarten, and although the whole grade had been in that group, I was closest to Misha. We even sat together at the same desk in the beginning, but then it quickly became clear that he was a future under-achiever and a troublemaker, and they separated us, proba-bly so that he didn't have a bad influence on me. They put me beside a girl who was a good student, potentially top of the class. But when they separated us in fifth grade she became a good student with the potential to be an aver-age one. They sat a new girl next to me, and the follow-ing year we were the first to be accepted into the Pioneers, because she was second-top of the class. Sensing something wasn't right, they moved her, and she barely finished school with Cs. The same pattern facilitated the descent and fall of a few more classmates, until, in the ninth grade, they sat me next to Dragon. Since he'd always had hopeless grades, could barely read, wrote even worse, and showed zero aca-demic ambition (and nobody would have believed it if he had tried), being my neighbor didn't affect his grades at all. Dragon was built of about one hundred kilograms of mus-cle, spent most of his school time training and competing in various competitions and championships. By the age of sixteen he had won everything there was to win, and so in the senior classes we started to see him more regularly. They sat him next to me, and the teachers gave him barely passing marks just because he wasn't skipping class and managed to blink his eyes in answer to questions.

But I wanted to write about Misha. Well, to be more precise, I'm still writing about myself, but in this bit I'll do that via Misha. In first grade they moved him away from me and sat him next to a simple girl, and they got Cs and Ds, very occasionally a B between the two of them, and they stuck together right up until ninth grade. Toward the end of our first school year, you could already tell who was going to do well, or rather was already doing well. But existence in hothouse conditions with the same teacher for the first four years somehow means there isn't much variation in the grades given to pupils, and you can't really judge the differences in their level of knowledge: everybody's quite close together, falling far behind only in especially difficult circumstances. All of infant school, I tried to fit in, and I more or less succeeded. I was one of the best, but that didn't really make me stand out, and it bothered nobody. The problems started when we burst out of the small world of one classroom into the wider world of the school and encountered other teachers. It quickly became clear that most of us were C students, with a few Bs (mostly girls) and a lot of Ds. There were catastrophically few A-grade students, and I turned out to be one of them. It wasn't that I was trying so hard to get high grades—I never studied all that hard and never bothered with learning stuff by heart, I just liked learning. I got used to doing well, and so studying was easy for me.

In fourth grade our class teacher was this older woman, a math teacher, and she seemed to decide I was a future Leonhard Euler or something, because she really adored me. The whole class decided I was her pet and that's why I was getting top marks and lots of praise, which she rarely gave to the others. She mostly grabbed boys by the scruff of the neck and dragged them round the class repeating the phrase "good-for-nothing" in various different intonations. Conflict was brewing, though unbeknownst to me. It all came out when, at the end of the year, I had a fight with Misha. He was smaller than me but naturally really strong and broad, while I for some reason was equally naturally thin and still not too tall. We hadn't been especially friendly before then, but neither had we been enemies. We fought over something stupid in the corridor during the break. Misha didn't even hit me, he just shoved me hard, so I fell against the radiator. I didn't cry, though it hurt. But that wasn't the problem—the problem was that the class teacher arrived just at the end of all this, saw what was going on, and, naturally, blamed it on Misha. He was already considered the undisputed leader of the class, and everyone reverentially called him Mikha, and so when he and his mother were summoned to speak to the headmaster, everybody, naturally, took his side, and I was branded a snitch. And then it started—hell started. For the next six months I was an outcast, the most despised creature in the class. In lessons, when the teacher was watching, everything was still fine, the worst that could happen would be a crack on the back of the head when she turned away. But what happened in the breaks is better forgotten about. And it wasn't the physical violence or humiliations that were so bad, but rather the constant and inescapable psychological bullying perpetrated by some with the willing connivance of others. It wasn't like everybody took turns beating me, but so many of them wanted to humiliate me, and no matter whom I fought, even if I won, which, with my frail build, was very rare, the whole class was always on the side of my opponent, and things just kept getting worse. I hid, ran away, defended myself as best I could but never complained and never asked for mercy. My main task was to survive somehow during the breaks and then slip out of school unnoticed. In every child collective there is a similar outcast, an untouchable, the object of general mockery and constant humiliation, whom every kid in the class ridicules, or, rather, some do, while the others just watch. This is hard to bear and impossible to change. It's worse than belonging to the wrong caste in India. All you can do is change schools or kill somebody, but I doubt the latter option would help.

This went on for almost five years, at first really intensely, and then later less so, more out of habit, but all the same . . . In class, in the corridor, in the changing room, in the sports hall, in the canteen, in the toilet, in the park behind the school, everywhere. Five years of hell. I never told my mum anything, but she could tell, and a few times, especially at the beginning, she suggested I could change schools. That meant traveling to another village every morning, and it meant giving in. But that wasn't even the main thing. I just wanted to be like everybody else: despite all the bullying, I wanted to be accepted. But somehow it just didn't work out. I was still the best student, a smart kid with an excellent memory, and my teachers still regularly threw me out of the class for arguing, but the class didn't consider me a human being. I tried smoking, gambling for money with the boys, but I could never get accepted, I was always on the sidelines, and far below. New kids came to the class, they went through the difficult process of initiation, some quickly, some slowly, with their own humiliations and fights, but they never ended up in the position of the last kid in the class, because that place was occupied. By me.

It's easy for me now to give my younger self advice: fight harder, and fight to the end, and don't just defend yourself, go to another school after all, or become the best at something, better than everyone else, to make them respect you (studying didn't count for much on that front). But I can see all that now. Then, and the same is true for any eleven-year-old kid in that situation today, there was nothing that could be done. The only way out is to become like everyone else, to let your studies slip, not stick out, to constantly give in, then maybe you'll get a slot in the leader's inner circle. But that wasn't the fate I wanted, I wanted to be accepted, but I also wanted to be myself, and that, for some reason, wasn't possible. So I just had to suffer and wait. Maybe that's why I became so introverted and stubborn? Maybe. But I don't think that was the only reason. Many other things, good and bad, happened to me in those years. And everything comes to an end eventually. Eventually, the bullying stopped, everyone grew up a bit, relationships got reshuffled, and by ninth grade nobody bothered me anymore; I started to become friends with a few of my classmates, and then with a lot of them, even with my old enemies. A lot of the fair-to-middling students went off to technical schools and colleges, and the only ones that were left were the brainy kids and the dunces, the former preparing for university, the latter for the army. We got merged with another class, and life changed completely . . .

We formed our own little group, and the last two years flew by as though in some kind of wonderous dream, probably as compensation for the black years of social exile. My studies didn't exactly suffer, but I now went to school less for knowledge and more for fun. Although I was still one of the best students, or, rather, the best male student (there were a couple of stronger female students), I did end up with a couple of Bs, so they suggested I resit the exams in order to get a medal. I declined, because I didn't really understand why I would need a medal, and I still don't. At the "last bell"— the last day of school—I carried a little girl from first grade on my shoulders (by seventeen I had gotten taller and stronger) and in her hands she held that same little bell with the nut on the string inside. I warned her that she should hold the bell part pointing downwards, and the thing rang a lot more joyously this time.

After the last bell came the final exams, five of them, which I, naturally, passed with straight As. The last one was mathematics, which I still wasn't in love with, but had remained faithful to throughout school. In the first twenty minutes I solved the first four problems, and then sat staring at a question about triangles for half an hour and eventually understood that I wouldn't crack it and that I'd end up with four out of five points. I started to sweat and wipe my brow, but, as usual, that didn't help. Fifteen minutes before the end of the exam it became clear that everybody was stuck on these triangles, including the other two A-grade girls, and that nobody was getting five out of five. Our original class teacher had retired by then, and in her absence we'd passed among various teachers, which meant that we ended up with a new math teacher for our final year. Seeing the situation at her own final exam, she called the three of us who had always passed everything with full marks out into the corridor, one by one, and, without a word, showed us the solution to the last problem. At first, I couldn't understand why someone from the examination commission was asking me to come out into the corridor. I was already stressed about not being able to defeat those triangles, and there was little time left, so I wanted to focus on the problem, but of course I went, since the authorities were asking me to. Having seen the solution and understood it, I went back to my place, thinking as I went. I was wearing a white shirt, and everyone around me was wearing white and generally all dressed-up, but suddenly I had this feeling that everything was fake and dirty. I sat down, and my first thought was to leave the problem unsolved, or, even better, to write something obscene instead of the solution, my final message to my teachers, as it were. But I didn't have the guts. I wanted to have five beautiful As after my final exams, I wanted to be, or rather, to retain my place as one of the best. And do it at any price. So I wrote the correct answer. And I got my A, my fifth, and last. But it didn't make me happy. Neither then, nor now. I had lost the chance to earn a deserved B and exchanged it for a dishonest A.

At our graduation, everybody applauded, and I applauded. I was the first to receive my diploma, as the best student, and they even made some kind of speech about my "great height and my future great deeds," but it made me feel sick.

I finished school and started studying at university, on a state-funded scholarship, in a prestigious college—all on the strength of my own brain. There was a lot of corruption there, and it was very tough for a mere mortal from a village to get in, but I managed. I was the very last name on the list of those who had graduated from high school with a "gold medal," but I managed. Before that, my relatives had suggested I move to another city, where I was guaranteed to get into an institute that I didn't like for a degree that I wasn't interested in. I refused. I wanted to go to the institute that my parents didn't want me to go to, where it would be almost impossible to succeed. I didn't listen to anyone, did what I wanted, and got my own way. For sure, after just half a year, after my first exams, I was already completely disappointed with our school, where the students pretended to study and the teachers pretended to teach, and I gave up on studying, suddenly became a bad student, skipped class, broke the rules, and spent five fabulous years within the walls of that institution, but that's another story entirely.

My school education wasn't wasted on me, it did actually teach me a thing or two— and I don't mean how to work out problems involving triangles, that never helped me. I learned never to give up and never to waste my energy on pointless stuff. Never give up, never waste energy. Never give up. Never waste energy. And also—that you really don't have to try to be like everyone else.

Testament

We are all going to die. And I, unfortunately, am no exception. We'd all like to live a bit longer, and here I, fortunately, am also no exception. No, I don't want to extend my life in order to live to a hundred and spend the last quarter of it dragging out my decrepit existence on various machines and drugs. I want to live my young, full life a bit longer, to receive pleasure from life and to give pleasure to others, to walk, or even better to run, to sleep at night or not sleep, and I want to be the one who decides all of this, not my organism and my doctors.

This is the kind of life I'd like to live for a bit longer. But it's not possible. We are all going to die. After death, we will all turn into lumps of rotting meat, buried a couple of meters underground. The worms will eat us, and our dutiful relatives will visit our graves, wear sad expressions on their faces, stand in front of the cross or gravestone, look at our portraits, forgetting entirely that crosses are planted at the feet of the departed, so the whole mournful company is now standing on his head and gazing tenderly at the portrait etched into the granite. Then they'll get their supplies and booze out and make sure everyone has a drink, including the deceased, of whom there won't be much left by that time, and the flowers will bloom all around.

I don't want people trampling on my head, even after I'm dead, and I don't want my children and grandchildren to remember me as a portrait on a slab of granite. I don't want a wake on my grave. I generally don't like drawing attention to myself, not now, and certainly not after I'm dead. I don't want a grave.

•

When I was a child, just four years old, I went to my grandfather's funeral. Usually, children don't remember themselves being that young, and only very occasionally do they remember the most remarkable events from that time. But I remember that funeral. I don't remember much, but I remember the main thing: me standing at the edge of the grave on a pile of dirt together with my relatives. And then, after the funeral, I was stunned to discover that they wouldn't be digging granddad up again, that he had died and that was it, forever. Throughout my whole childhood I had a recurring nightmare: in the evening or during the night I would see a black grave and a body in a white shroud being lowered into it. It was granddad's body, but I imagined that it was me, and I knew that sooner or later it would be. Never take your children to a funeral.

As a child, I was afraid that I would die. Now I'm not afraid—now I know that I'll die. As a child, I was afraid of the darkness of the grave, but now I just don't want to lie in it.

We are all going to die. Each in our own way. Some will die quietly, as though closing the door to the bedroom of a child who has only just fallen asleep. Others will die in cries and suffering, as though during birth. I don't know how I will die, but I definitely don't want to die as a decrepit old man in bed surrounded by yawning relatives.

There was once a man who was asked how he would like to die, and he answered: "With a shout of 'hurrah!' on my lips, a gun slung over my shoulder, and a mouth full of blood." I'd also like that—it's beautiful, it's manly. But that's not how it works. Heroes die beautifully only in movies and books. In real life, they piss blood into their pants, scream from pain, and remember their mothers.

I don't want a grave. I want to be burned. No, not on the bonfire of some inquisition, but in a simple crematorium. Burned, and the ashes sprinkled at sea. If possible, on the Black Sea, and in summer, when the sun is shining and a fresh wind is blowing. But even if it's autumn and raining, that's also not so bad. I wouldn't want you waiting for summer if I kick the bucket in November. Otherwise you'll have guests round asking, "What have you got in that vase there?" "That's our granddad, he's waiting for summer!" The vase should also go into the sea, by the way— no need to fetishize it. Otherwise, that same room, a year later, different guests will ask, "What's that vase you've got there?" "Granddad was in that vase," the relatives will announce, solemnly getting to their feet. In that case, why don't we hang my socks and underpants around the house then—my favorite ones, and the ones I wore last?

I want to be burned. To ashes. And the ashes to be spread on the wind. On the sea. Best in summer, if, of course, I die in summer. Just remember to throw the ashes on the wind away from the boat, so that they are blown over the sea and

74

not onto the boat, so that some cheeky grandchild (clearly taking after his granddad) won't be tempted to comment, as he sweeps up my remains, "Nothing but problems with that old guy!"

Let the wind take my ashes out to sea. But if it's raining, that's okay. They'll all say, "That means we're burying a good man, since it's raining." But you're not burying— you're sowing, friends, that is, blowing!

And if it's raining and the ashes get a bit stuck to the urn, that's also fine. True, that same cheeky grandchild will look into the urn, see a bit of leftover ashes and say, "Yeah, granddad's still hanging on!" But that's fine, just throw the urn into the sea too. So that there's nothing left. Nothing at all. Just memory. And the things I did. And my friends. And you. And then I'll always be with you.

Grandma

I had a grandmother and I didn't like her. It happens.

•

It also might happen that you're born a woman, you live in a small village, you work your whole life, of your four children only one survives, your husband eventually leaves you for another woman, and you're left alone. Okay, not entirely alone—with a child. The child then grows up, goes off to study, then to the army, then gets married, and goes to live far away and forever. And then you're left entirely alone. I can't imagine how all this would feel, and I don't want to.

•

Your son visits very rarely, brings a grandson or granddaughter. But their visits are short and reluctant. Then you hit sev-
enty, your son comes to visit for the last time, you sell the old
wooden house and move in with him, into a stone house
far away. Apart from your son, your grandson, your granddaughter, and your son's wife live there. They're not pleased
to have you there. They're not mean to you, they put up
with you, it's called "caring for an elderly parent."

The room is separate and new, but the things in it are
all old, from the wooden house. The room quickly absorbs
the smell of old age. They bring you your pension on time,
nobody wants to take it away from you, they never even ask,
and you can spend it however you like. How you like is usually on grocery shopping, sometimes you give some to your
son's wife—there's never enough money in any family and
this family is no exception. The rest goes into your savings
book, like it should. You do it, the family you live with does
it. That's the best way, it's safer.

Every other day they bring you newspapers, you can
read them. Sometimes they invite you to come and watch
television in the living room. They make food for you
regularly. On Saturday, they go to the bathhouse and "do
you need anything washed?" In the evening you can pray,

kneeling in your old nightgown. At night, you urinate into a one-liter jar—it's too cold and dark to go to the outside toilet. You can also write letters to grandmas just like you who live far away and sometimes get replies. As the years pass, the letters are sent and received less and less frequently.

All of these activities take up most of your time. The rest of the time you can sit in your room and look out the window. You can see everything: who comes, who goes, who came through the gate from that direction, who left in that direction, who walked along the street, who drove along it. True, you can't see the street so well, you have a better view of the gate, but the window is big, with curtains. You can hide behind them sometimes, so nobody can see that you're watching everybody.

•

Twelve years passed like that. Twelve years . . . For twelve years my grandmother and I lived in the same house. What did I know about her? Nothing. What did she know about me? Even less. Did we speak to each other? Yes. About what? Nothing. She'd pester me with her old-folks' conversations, but I wasn't interested in them and I'd try to avoid them, or I'd just leave the room. She wasn't very smart, a bit unpleasant, quite fat and old, and I didn't love her. Did she love me? I don't know. I didn't think about it then, I was young, skinny, sometimes smart, and reasonably polite, so I wasn't mean to her and I put up with her. And secretly made fun of her. Everybody in our family made fun of her, and we often got annoyed with her, for a good reason or otherwise. She didn't exactly suffer with us, but she wasn't happy either.

•

Her granddaughter got married and moved out and soon had a baby, her great-grandchild. Her granddaughter and her husband lived nearby and came round often with the baby in the pram. The child was still very small and so was always sleeping, but grandma still carried her stool out of her room and put it down next to the pram. This was called "caring for the grandchildren." Then the child got bigger, and her son's wife began to look after him—they joked about her new status and now started calling her grandma. And the old grandma was no longer entrusted with her great-grandchild. They didn't entrust her with much in that house, in case she did something wrong and upset her son's wife. Nevertheless, grandma always managed to do something or other, and do it wrong, of course, and of course it upset her son's wife.

Every evening they'd have a conversation about washing up that was so well-worn it had practically become a ritual:

"Liusya, leave those, I'll wash up."

"I'll do it, there's nothing to wash."

And so it was every evening, every day, and in everything—quiet, wordless resentment and putting-up-with instead of respect and tolerance. But grandma didn't get offended. She grew up and lived her whole life in a village, read with difficulty, was simple, not too smart, a bit fat and old, and on top of that she was going deaf. Grandma was in good health, she was almost never ill, though she complained about her health a lot, especially about her heart, but nobody really worried about that too much.

And then one quiet summer's day her son died, and she sat on the bench in the garden of the stone house and cried, her eyes were red, and she kept clapping her hands on her lap. People came in the evening, lots of them, and comforted her. They comforted the whole family, including grandma, and she liked it that they were paying attention to her.

•

But life went on anyway. It didn't finish. Life never finishes, even if someone leaves it. Grandma started to forget things more—names and dates, the kettle on the hob, the tap or the gas. She didn't get ill more often, but she felt worse, she aged even more and started causing even more problems. Her grandson had long ago moved to the city, her great-grandson had grown up and was going to school, he was the least interested of all of them in grandma's business. She lived alone, or rather, with her son's wife, and she was already well past eighty. Her son's wife was also aging and getting ill, and she was finding it harder and less convenient to look after this superfluous and unloved person. A few more years passed like this, and the last one was full of phrases like: "She's no one to me now . . . I can't look after her anymore . . . She'll be better off there . . . My friend works there, it's a good place . . ."

There was no meeting and no vote, just silent consent. One day they gathered grandma and her things together and loaded them into a car. They said they were taking her to the hospital, which pleased grandma—she was already pretty far gone by then—and they took her to the old people's home.

They sent her pension there, gave them her documents, and that was it, grandma was gone.

I lived in the city where the old people's home was. I had already started a family, had kids. I rarely thought about my grandma, never asked about her and never wanted to see her. It was shameful and unpleasant. I didn't love her, she was old, a bit unpleasant, fat, and not too smart, I tried not to think about her and almost forgot about her. My mum visited her infrequently at first, and then stopped completely. She was no longer young herself now, she was old; and she was no longer healthy, but sick.

We didn't speak any more about grandma in our family. A few years passed and one day someone said she had died. Who said it and to whom weren't exactly clear, but nobody really wanted to figure out what had happened, and somehow we just carried on living. And then a few more years passed and one day out of the blue we got a call from the old people's home saying that grandma had died a long time ago already and asking if the relatives were going to bury her. The relatives answered that yes, they would, although they thought they'd been told that ... well, it doesn't matter, we'll get to that bit soon. The grandchildren went to get their grandmother from the old people's home. As soon as she saw the nurses drinking tea and eating chocolates in the staff room the granddaughter put on a mournful face and gave them our name and the reason we were there. The grandson went to the morgue to identify the body. They rolled her out on a trolley. She was lying on her side, very old, curled up and dried out. The grandson didn't recognize his grandmother, he recognized only the clothes. But he didn't say anything and helped the nurse move the very light body into the coffin. They nailed the lid on immediately. A hearse in the shape of a yellow bus with a black stripe down the side took grandma back to the village, to the earth, to her son. The grandson held on to the coffin so it didn't rattle around too much on the bus. The driver was in a rush, they dug the grave quickly, there was no one around, it was a gloomy November day.

•

I have another grandmother. She lives far, far away and is very, very old. I see her very rarely, but I at least see her, and I love her. She is old and capricious, but she's cheerful and kind. She's very small and thin. She is really old now, and really ill, she's not all there and causes a lot of problems. She lives with her daughter, that is, my aunt. My aunt is also old now, not young anymore, and sick, not healthy. They constantly argue. This is called "caring for grandma." Grandma's daughter's daughter's daughter also lives with them, in other words, her great granddaughter. This is called "looking after the grandchild." This is how they live together: the old, the very old, and the young.

My grandfather I saw only once. And the other grandfather I also saw only once, but that was in a photograph, but maybe it wasn't him, I'm not sure. Also, it's easy to love the person who is far away, but hard to love the person who is nearby. It's also easy to write about all this, but hard to do anything about it. Especially now.

The Makars

Makar lived on the other side of the fence from us. He was my neighbor and my best friend in childhood, one of those people you don't remember meeting, you've just known them forever. His name was Igor, he was quite strong and pretty fat. He already started getting a moustache in fourth grade, and by seventh it was all there. Makar was four years older than me. I never had a big brother—I had Makar. He taught me a lot. True, not much of that was useful, and even less was good. Makar wasn't a bully or a troublemaker, he was kind of quiet, he read a lot, mostly history stuff, but he wasn't a good student. He wasn't stupid, he was cunning, a bit of a rascal, though he didn't mean anyone any harm. Or that's how it looked from the outside. If you looked close up, at least from across the fence, then Makar was a pretty good friend. Despite the quite big, by kids' standards, age difference, we were really close—he was my protector, if not a particularly commanding one. But then his childhood finished, and they took him to the army, while mine kept going for a while.

But while our childhoods were still running in parallel, we did a lot of interesting things: we walked our dogs together in the forest, we played football and chizh, rode our bikes, swam in the pond, took used bits of wood and rubber bands to make rifles that shot bullets made from nails, and a whole load of other typical things that typical village kids do. He taught me to smoke and to play cards, at first just for fun, then for money. Makar was better than everyone else at trinka, and I, like many others, always lost to him, but I didn't lose much—because we never had much. Makar played really well, he was cunning, skillfully manipulating his opponents, and he always came out on top.

In winter, Makar and I even managed to played hockey! Mainly, we played football with the other kids, or just passed the ball to each other on the street or in his yard. On TV, however, apart from football, we also watched hockey, because we had both been bought hockey sticks just in case it ever snowed in Crimea and didn't melt before we got home from school. The sticks lay in our attics and store cupboards for a couple of years and then, finally, there was a beautiful fall of white and downy snow. We trampled out a little "rink" for ourselves in Makar's yard, put two benches at each end in place of goals, and started to play real hockey, with a puck, though not on skates, of course— a kind of running hockey. Everything was going great, we were scoring goals, the little rink was full of excitement, until I took an overenthusiastic swipe at the puck and whacked Makar, who was standing behind me, on the head with my stick. I barely even felt anything, but he yelled out "Ow! Ow!" and with has hand held over his bloodied brow he ran into the house. I stood alone for a while on our little ice rink, looked at the tiny, neat red spots on the white, well-trampled surface, and then slouched off home with my stick over my shoulder. We didn't play hockey again after that. I never even said sorry. And not because I'm so ill-mannered or insensitive. It's just that when you're a kid, a little boy, it isn't done, saying sorry. If you've done something wrong, like I did with that hockey stick, you just stand there, or you say something like: "Let's see!" or, "It's not so bad," or if what you've seen really does look pretty bad, then, "Should probably go to the hospital."

Between Makar's yard and ours there was a fence made of thick wire mesh, and we were always climbing over it to go visit each other. We could have gone via the gate, of course, but climbing the fence was somehow closer—both in terms of distance and in terms of simple human relations. Makar climbed the fence only rarely, because the wire mesh really wasn't designed to hold hundred-kilogram loads, but I was light and skinny and would jump across several times a day. The fence had bent and sagged in the place where we would climb across, and I got yelled at for that, but I refused to give up the direct route to my friend. Since Makar rarely made the trip across the fence, if he needed me, he would just come up to the fence and shout. I'd come running, and we'd often stand there for ages talking. Boys somehow can't talk to one another just like that, they have to have some business to discuss, it might be something small, but it'll be important for them. We could talk like that for a long time.

I'll never forget how I once ran from my gate to Makar's fence to get his advice about a deal on micromotors. Micromotors were these little motors that had been ripped out of old Soviet electronic devices. Smart kids could use them, in combination with some batteries, to make little toy cars. At that time, all we had were toy cars that you had to push along yourself. You can't imagine what a battery-powered car meant for a seven-year-old village kid back then!

An unachievable dream! That kid couldn't even have imagined that there existed such a thing as remote-controlled
cars (the ones on a wire, never mind the radio-controlled
ones) or that one might even dream of such things. So the
most inventive kids made cars for themselves. Or with their
dads' help, it didn't matter—the main thing was that boys
like this and their toy cars existed. And so, one day, two of
these happy little boys with one of these little cars in their
hands came to call on even littler me. They'd found out from
somewhere that I'd got two excellent new micromotors. I
think I knew one of the boys and had said something to
him about it myself—it wasn't like they would have been
spying on me, after all. It doesn't matter—the main thing
is they showed up and wanted my micromotors, and at the
same time I was dreaming of a battery-powered car, or at
least a set of plastic Hungarian soldiers, Indians, or at least
cowboys. I already had pirates, and there was no point in
dreaming of Vikings, they were impossible to get hold of. So
when the two boys asked me to give them the micromotors, just like that, I told them I would have to think about
it. I left them sitting on the bench by the gate and ran to the
fence to call Makar for advice. Makar was a person of experience—he was a fourth grader after all, and so had basically

already lived half his life— and, after a moment's consideration, he suggested that I ask for a real battery-powered car, or, at the very least, twenty Vikings in exchange for the two micromotors. I ran back to the gate. The boys calmly listened to our proposition and said that they had nothing to give me, but they showed me how their homemade car worked. Only very small boys with very active imaginations could call the thing crawling along my bench a car, and even then, you'd have to look at it from a certain angle—from a low vantage point, as it crawled toward you. But I was precisely one of those boys, and the thing wobbling along the wooden bench made an indelible impression on me, so I ran back to the fence. I ran back and forth like this for about an hour, during which Makar and I gradually lowered our demands to ten Indians or, say, two of these homemade cars. Makar clearly wanted to stay in the background of the negotiations, but I'm sure he would have been counting on fifty percent of any proceeds. But the boys told me that in the time I'd been running back and forth across the yard they hadn't come into any more soldiers, and that exchanging two micromotors for two finished cars, for which the motors were the main but certainly not the only component, made little sense. Whether it made sense for me to just give my motors away to them for nothing, they didn't say, and I didn't ask. In the end, the deal fell through, and the motors, which had now shot up in value in my eyes, got left out in the rain at some point, swelled up and went rusty, and ended up in the bin. A year later, on my birthday, I was given a remote-controlled tank, which was operated via a meter-long wire, which was a bit short, but, on the other hand, was useful for yanking it whenever it happened to get stuck. The tank didn't go outside, it was for indoor use only.

Makar had a big family. His parents, Uncle Misha and Auntie Katya, were proper village Ukrainians, with the characteristic accent and manners, and they had moved to Crimea from somewhere in mainland Ukraine. They were all quite fat, especially Auntie Katya, and they were proper collective farm folks, despite the fact that she anyway had worked all her life in the city, in some big factory, where she went every day on the bus, despite her sick legs. Uncle Misha was fat, but not quite as voluminous as his wife, he just had a big belly, which he waddled around behind. Although he didn't walk much, because he worked as a truck driver and spent more and more time behind the wheel. Makar also had an older sister and an older brother. The sister was called Svetka, she was five years older than

Makar, pretty stupid and not too pretty. Her most distinctive physical feature were her blackheads, which she was always squeezing, and which she could thus never get rid of. But Svetka wanted to be a singer. She was a huge fan of Sofia Rotaru and wanted to go off and study wherever they train singers. When my cousins, two girls, came to visit us for the summer and heard about Svetka's ambitions, they naturally jumped at the chance to test her talents, to help prepare her for her entrance exams. Late in the evening, Svetka put on a concert, standing on her side of the fence, while on our side our two little mischief-makers lay on the ground under the bushes choking with laughter – it wasn't possible to listen to Svetka singing and stay standing upright. The examination commission at the place where they train singers (though not all singers, as it turned out) reacted in pretty much the same way to Svetka, and in the end she went to work in the factory like her mother. These days the TV is full of all kinds of tone-deaf idiots with neither a decent voice nor an ear for music trying to get on various shows, but then such a phenomenon was a rarity.

Makar's elder brother, Valerka, also wasn't the sharpest tool in the box—uneducated, untalented, but at the same time unambitious. After military service he went straight into the collective farm and worked as a driver, like his dad. He married a local teacher, had two children with her—a smart girl with a huge birthmark that covered half her face and an unremarkable boy.

In our family, the weekends rarely differed much from weekdays, but in Makar's house the whole family would get together and things would often get really noisy. I wouldn't say that we were good friends with Makar's family, like it sometime is in cities when families call round on each other a lot or maybe go away somewhere on holiday together. In the village, good neighbors live like one family, only with a fence between them and with their own money hidden in their own pillows. They're not neighbors, but one big clan. That's how things were between our families.

I knew Makar my whole life, and I knew that was his nickname, which was derived from his surname, and when I grew up, I was surprised to learn that adults also had nicknames. Makar's dad, Uncle Misha, was also called "Makar" by his friends—they had the same surname, after all, and adults are just kids who've grown up a bit but often still think in the same way.

The Makars always ate well. Or, rather, not so much well, as just a lot. That's probably more like it—they just ate a lot. Auntie Katya would always go by the shops on the way home from work and come home with enormous bags—if she bought bread, it would be six loaves, if it was milk, then the same number of big glass bottles. So everybody in the family was well-fed, and the most overfed of the lot was, of course, Makar—my Makar. He was bigger than his father and bigger than his brother and at eighteen, before he went to the army, he looked like he was pushing thirty.

When Makar had to go to the army—this was in 1990, a year before the collapse of the Soviet Union— for some reason he was sent off to serve in the Russian Far East. His parents found out that their son was being sent to the other end of the country, that he'd be flying on a normal civilian airplane with the other conscripts, and that they could come to the airport to say goodbye. They found this out at the very last minute, and since they didn't have their own car, we went in ours. Auntie Katya packed two bags full of food, and we set off, together with my dad. Whether we got the time wrong or were late because of preparing the food, I don't know, but when we got to the airport there was no sign of the conscripts or of Makar. I ran up to the first floor to look at the crowd down below and try to find my friend that way, but all I could see was Uncle Misha and Auntie Katya desperately searching for their son in the public part of the airport outside the departure area. Uncle Misha, with his belly and waddling gait, strode among the passengers, and Auntie Katya with her fat, swollen legs, minced through the crowd with her two big bags, in which, alongside all their homemade food, she had surely stashed some cigarettes and a bottle of moonshine. But Makar was nowhere to be found, he'd already gone. After a lot of wandering round the airport and shrugging our shoulders, we drove home.

And then the Soviet Union cracked and disintegrated, and the lives of many cracked and disintegrated along with it. Life got tough for almost everybody, including us and the Makars. But somehow it was tougher for them. Svetka was unhappily married—she'd married a guy from a small town who seemed, on the outside, normal, and was even pretty good-looking, unlike Svetka herself, but things went badly. He turned out to be unbalanced and suffering from some kind of nervous disorder. I only saw him a couple of times and once stood behind him in a queue for bread, where I watched him for a long time as he constantly twitched his head and shoulders for no reason, and you could see that something wasn't quite right with him. Then he started to drink, to beat Svetka, and to regularly throw her out of the house. She'd show up every so often at her parents with her little daughter, sometimes with a car loaded with her stuff, sometimes with nothing. Things continued in this way until her daughter grew up a bit and came to live with her grandma Katya permanently. Her granddaughter was big, a typical Makar, but she was neither pretty nor smart. Life is especially tough for girls who are neither pretty nor smart. And Svetka sailed off to her husband, or somewhere else on her own, visiting her daughter more and more rarely.

Valerka started drinking. In Makar's family, just like in all the other families, they drank—when there's no work and no money it becomes the main way of passing the time. It doesn't look good, and it doesn't smell good. His wife left him with the kids. First they came to our town, and then they moved on to another one, bigger and farther away. Valerka also went to the city soon after that, trying to make at least some kind of wage—there had been no work in the village for ages—but he didn't last long anywhere. The wages were bad, and he already had a serious drinking habit to feed.

Uncle Misha also drank, but he did so in resolute binges. About five years later he got really sick—it was the sugar, they said. After another two years, he was confined to his bed, and after another year he died, quietly, in his bed, next to the stove, already several times smaller than he used to be.

Makar himself, as soon as the big country collapsed, disappeared from his unit, stealing some supplies before he went. It took him a few months to get home from Khabarovsk, trading whatever he'd managed to take with him from the army and whatever else fell into his hands. At first, they looked for him, but later, when it became clear that Ukraine was already a different country, they gave up— but it meant he couldn't get himself a passport. When Makar finally got home—thinner, with a weathered face, with the traces of boils still on his arms—I hardly recognized him. He'd grown up and changed dramatically, and not only in his appearance. I had also changed, maybe not as much, but still. We met at the fence, talked about something for a bit, and then parted.

Makar filled out on his mum's cooking, and pretty soon disappeared again, this time from his own home. For about a year, nobody heard from him. Somebody caught sight of him in the city at the market, and, seeing how he was dressed, immediately assumed he was now a gangster. Although at that time anyone who didn't look homeless or like he lived in the village was assumed to be in the mafia.

But Makar was never that way inclined, and, knowing how much he liked gambling, money, and wheeling and dealing, I reckoned that must be how he was making a living. And a year later I met him myself at the train station. I was late for the train home and was walking quickly along the platform. He was also in a hurry, but going in the opposite direction. We walked past each other in the small, crowded station concourse and didn't recognize each other at first. But then, at the same moment, we both stopped and turned around. Makar was more like a tramp now than a villager; in any case, I, a poor first-year student, looked like a real dandy compared with him. Something had clearly changed dramatically, for the umpteenth time in his life, and, judging by the downtrodden look on his face, he didn't really want to talk about it, and I was in a hurry, so we stood for a couple of seconds, ten meters apart, and looked at each other, then went our separate ways.

A few years later Makar came back home to his mum. In the village, he drank like everyone else, ran up debts, and disappeared regularly. When he was gone, his debtors would visit. Auntie Katya paid them off at first, while she still could, and then she just cried. By that time her legs were really bad, the factory had been closed down, her pension was peanuts, and she had to walk a lot—in winter, she'd go to the forest for firewood, because they had never had gas put in, they couldn't afford it, and coal wasn't free either, and if you don't heat the stove life gets pretty cold. In summer she gathered rosehip and dogwood and other things in the forest, worked on other people's allotments and grew things in her own, and took it all on the train to the market in town, which, like the road to the forest, wasn't exactly just a short stroll down the street . . . She scraped some money together, she fed herself and her granddaughter, and Makar if he was home. And she did a lot of other things besides. All that was left of the old, blooming, kind Auntie Katya was a headscarf and the painful legs of an old woman. I don't know what color her eyes were, I tried not to look into them.

Makar was still alright at that point, more or less still presentable, and he even managed to get married a couple of times. The ladies, of course, were no picnic, but they were good drinking buddies. I heard something about a kid that died young, but I don't really know the full story. Makar slowly drank himself into decline. The ladies, even the least sought-after ones, no longer looked his way. He tried to earn a bit of money where he could—his mother couldn't always help him out and nobody would lend him anything.

Once on a winter night, somewhere not in our village, I think it was in the city, he got drunk, froze out on the street, and ended up losing his legs. In the hospital they cut them off at the knee because of the onset of gangrene. They kept him in for a long time, and then for a long time nobody was able to transport him home, and then he lay in bed at home, and then, eventually, he left the house and started to hobble around the streets on his healed-up stumps. He couldn't register himself for disabled benefits, because he'd never managed to get himself a passport after the army, and he even stopped drinking so much for a while.

I didn't visit the village often then, but one time I did run into him. I just happened to have managed to buy myself a good car, and it wasn't the most pleasant experience to drive it through our village with the spiteful locals looking at it as though I'd personally stolen it from them—and then to top it all off I met Makar. He was tottering pretty boisterously down the street and I was driving toward him. I stopped, and he came up to the car. The window was open, Makar leaned on the door, and we said hello. With me sitting in the driving seat and him on his half-legs, our faces were on the same level. I was pretty shaken by this and didn't know what to say. Makar lit up a cigarette, said something nice, and we immediately fell silent. He was squinting into the summer sun, and we had nothing to say to each other, just like that time at the station, or even earlier, that time by the fence. We stood like that for a while, and then I drove off, and he went on his way, with his new, swinging, cut-off gait.

But in the end Makar didn't stop drinking, and some-time toward winter he fell asleep drunk somewhere again and this time died for good. I don't know if Auntie Katya mourned him, I wasn't there then, but her face didn't change much, it had been pretty scary to look at for a long time already, and now it just got even blacker.

Her last granddaughter grew up and, having only just finished 9th grade, moved out. Valerka and Svetka pretty much stopped visiting her. A few years passed, and Auntie Katya also died. Our neighbor came running in and said Auntie Katya was sick. When they came to have a look at her it was plain that she wasn't sick, she just didn't care anymore.

Their house is empty and dilapidated now, the garden is overgrown, and the trees have dried up; the water and elec-tricity were cut off a long time ago. Some family tried to move in there, but everything was so rotten inside that it was impossible to rescue it, and of course they had no money for it, so they left. They say Valerka wants to come back from the city, but somehow I don't believe it, and he couldn't live in the house anyway.

But the fence is still there, and it's still bent and sagging in the same place, there's just nobody to climb over and visit anymore.

OLEG SENTSOV is a Ukranian film director, screenwriter, and author from Simferopol, Crimea, in Ukraine, who first came to international prominence following the release of his 2011 film, *Gamer*. Sentsov was arrested in his hometown by Russian occupying forces in May 2014 on dubious charges after participating in the Euromaidan demonstrations that led to the overthrow of former Ukrainian President Viktor Yanukovych, and after helping to deliver supplies to trapped Ukrainian troops during Russia's occupation of Crimea. He was sentenced to twenty years in prison after a farcical show trial, causing an outcry by international human rights groups who condemned his imprisonment as a fabrication by the Russian government in an attempt to silence dissent; these organizations called for investigations into reports that Sentsov was tortured and witnesses coerced.

SENTSOV's prolific creative works includes two books of short stories; several scripts, plays, essays; one feature film; and two short films: *A Perfect Day for Bananafish* and *The Horn of the Bull*. In 2016, Sentsov was awarded the Taras Shevchenko National Prize of Ukraine, the country's highest honor for artistic achievement, and in 2017 he received the PEN/Barbey Freedom to Write Award. In May of 2018, he began a 145-day hunger strike to protest the incarceration of Ukrainian political prisoners in Russia, which led the European Parliament to award him the Sakharov Prize for Freedom of Thought. As this edition was going to press in September 2019, Sentsov was one of thirty-five Ukrainian political prisoners released in a prisoner swap with Russia. He is now back in Ukraine, where he plans to continue making movies and writing, while advocating for the release of all remaining Ukrainian political prisoners in Russia.

DR. UILLEAM BLACKER is an academic and translator specializing in Ukrainian, Polish, and Russian literature. His translations of contemporary Ukrainian literature have appeared in numerous publications, including *Modern Poetry in Translation*, *Words Without Borders*, and Dalkey Archive's *Best European Fiction* series.

Thank you all
for your support.
We do this for you,
and could not do
it without you.

DEEP
VELLUM

PARTNERS

pixel ||| texel

ADDITIONAL DONORS, CONT'D

Grace Kenney
JJ Italiano
Joseph Milazzo
Kelly Falconer
Laura Thomson
Lea Courington
Leigh Ann Pike
Lowell Frye
Maaza Mengiste
Mark Haber
Mary Cline
Maynard Thomson
Michael Reklis
Mike Soto

Mokhtar Ramadan
Nikki & Dennis Gibson
Patrick Kukucka
Patrick Kutcher
Rev. Elizabeth & Neil Moseley
Richard Meyer
Scott & Katy Nimmons
Sherry Perry
Stephen Harding
Susan Carp
Susan Ernst
Theater Jones
Tim Perttula
Tony Thomson

SUBSCRIBERS

Audrey Golosky
Brandon Kennedy
Caroline West
Chana Porter
Charles Dee Mitchell
Chris Mullikin
Chris Sweet
Courtney Sheedy
Damon Copeland
Daniel Kushner
Devin McComas
Elisabeth Cook
Francisco Fiallo
Hillary Richards
Jerry Hawkins
Jody Sims
Joe Milazzo

John Winkelman
Lance Stack
Lesley Conzelman
Martha Gifford
Michael Binkley
Michael Elliott
Michael Lighty
Michael Sorrel
Neal Chuang
Patricia Fels
Ryan Todd
Samuel Herrera
Shelby Vincent
Stephanie Barr
Steve Jansen
William Pate

AVAILABLE NOW FROM DEEP VELLUM

MICHÈLE AUDIN · *One Hundred Twenty-One Days*
translated by Christiana Hills · FRANCE

BAE SUAH · *Recitation*
translated by Deborah Smith · SOUTH KOREA

EDUARDO BERTI · *The Imagined Land*
translated by Charlotte Coombe · ARGENTINA

CARMEN BOULLOSA · *Texas: The Great Theft* · *Before* · *Heavens on Earth*
translated by Samantha Schnee · Peter Bush · Shelby Vincent · MEXICO

Cleave, Sarah, ed. · *Banthology: Stories from Banned Nations* · IRAN, IRAQ,
LIBYA, SOMALIA, SUDAN, SYRIA & YEMEN

LEILA S. CHUDORI · *Home*
translated by John H. McGlynn · INDONESIA

DOROTA MASŁOWSKA · *Honey, I Killed the Cats*
translated by Benjamin Paloff · POLAND

ANANDA DEVI · *Eve Out of Her Ruins*
translated by Jeffrey Zuckerman · MAURITIUS

ALISA GANIEVA · *Bride and Groom* · *The Mountain and the Wall*
translated by Carol Apollonio · RUSSIA

ANNE GARRÉTA · *Sphinx* · *Not One Day*
translated by Emma Ramadan · FRANCE

JÓN GNARR · *The Indian* · *The Pirate* · *The Outlaw*
translated by Lytton Smith · ICELAND

KIM YIDEUM · *Blood Sisters*
translated by Ji yoon Lee · SOUTH KOREA

GOETHE · *The Golden Goblet: Selected Poems*
translated by Zsuzsanna Ozsváth and Frederick Turner · GERMANY

NOEMI JAFFE · *What are the Blind Men Dreaming?*
translated by Julia Sanches & Ellen Elias-Bursac · BRAZIL

CLAUDIA SALAZAR JIMÉNEZ · *Blood of the Dawn*
translated by Elizabeth Bryer · PERU

JUNG YOUNG MOON · *Vaseline Buddha*
translated by Yewon Jung · SOUTH KOREA

JOSEFINE KLOUGART · *Of Darkness*
translated by Martin Aitken · DENMARK

FORTHCOMING FROM DEEP VELLUM

ANNE GARRÉTA · *In/concrete*
translated by Emma Ramadan · FRANCE

C.F. RAMUZ · *Jean-Luc Persecuted*
translated by Olivia Baes · SWITZERLAND

DMITRY LIPSKEROV · *The Tool and the Butterflies*
translated by Reilly Costigan-Humes & Isaac Stackhouse Wheeler · RUSSIA

FOWZIA KARIMI · *Above Us the Milky Way: An Illuminated Alphabet* · USA

GORAN PETROVIĆ · *At the Lucky Hand, aka The Sixty-Nine Drawers*
translated by Peter Agnone · SERBIA

JESSICA SCHIEFAUER · *Girls Lost*
translated by Saskia Vogel · SWEDEN

JUNG YOUNG MOON · *Seven Samurai Swept Away in a River*
translated by Yewon Jung · SOUTH KOREA

LEYLA ERBIL · *A Strange Woman*
translated by Nermin Menemencioğlu · TURKEY

MAGDA CARNECI · *FEM*
translated by Sean Cotter · ROMANIA

MARIO BELLATIN · *Mrs. Murakami's Garden*
translated by Heather Cleary · MEXICO

MATHILDE CLARK · *Lone Star*
translated by Martin Aitken · DENMARK

MÄRTA TIKKANEN · *The Love Story of the Century*
translated by Stina Katchadourian · FINLAND

MIKE SOTO · *A Grave Is Given Supper: Poems* · USA

MIRCEA CĂRTĂRESCU · *Solenoid*
translated by Sean Cotter · ROMANIA

PERGENTINO JOSÉ · *Red Ants: Stories*
translated by Tom Bunstead and the author · MEXICO

TAISIA KITAISKAIA · *The Nightgown & Other Poems* · USA

TATIANA RYCKMAN · *The Ancestry of Objects* · USA